THIS WALKER BOOK
BELONGS TO:

THIS BOOK

S.y, Kaina

mirzza

D0480845

LONDON BOROUGH OF RICHMOND UPON THAMES	
90710 000 469 736	
Askews & Holts	14-Apr-2021
JF	
RTWH	

'B' is for Bob

E.McL.

First published 2020 by Walker Books Ltd
87 Vauxhall Walk, London SE11 5HJ

This edition published 2021

2 4 6 8 10 9 7 5 3 1

Text © 2020 Eoin McLaughlin
Illustrations © 2020 Marc Boutavant

The right of Eoin McLaughlin and Marc Boutavant to be identified as author
and illustrator respectively of this work has been asserted by them
in accordance with the Copyright, Designs and Patents Act 1988

This book has been typeset in Clarendon

Printed and bound in China

All rights reserved. No part of this book may be reproduced, transmitted
or stored in an information retrieval system in any form or by any means,
graphic, electronic or mechanical, including photocopying, taping and
recording, without prior written permission from the publisher.

British Library Cataloguing in Publication Data:
a catalogue record for this book is available from the British Library

ISBN 978-1-4063-9075-9

www.walker.co.uk

not AN ALPHABET BOOK
THE CASE OF THE MISSING CAKE

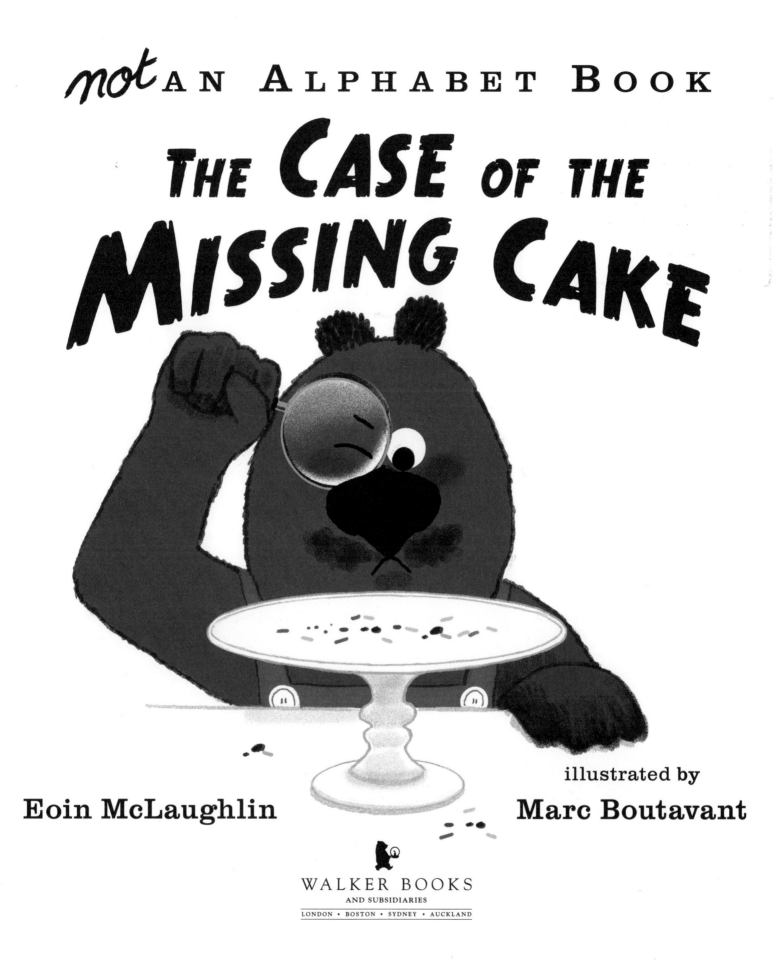

Eoin McLaughlin

illustrated by
Marc Boutavant

WALKER BOOKS
AND SUBSIDIARIES
LONDON • BOSTON • SYDNEY • AUCKLAND

Oh! Thank *goodness* you're here! This was meant to be a simple alphabet book but something **horrible** has happened. The most *terrible* crime! The world's most completely delicious, tongue-jinglingly, chocolaty cake has been ... STOLEN!

1

Oh, you should've seen it, it was filled with cream and sprinkled

with sprinkles and just sitting on Page 5, but now

if you turn there you can see it's

GONE...

Won't you help me find the
thief? They're somewhere
right here in this book.

A is for Apple.

Good day to you, Mr Apple. Did you steal the cake?

Hmmm ... no comment.

B is for Bear.

This is my page. Move along. Nothing to see here.

C is for Cake.

GONE!

D is for Dog.

Are you the cake thief, Dog?

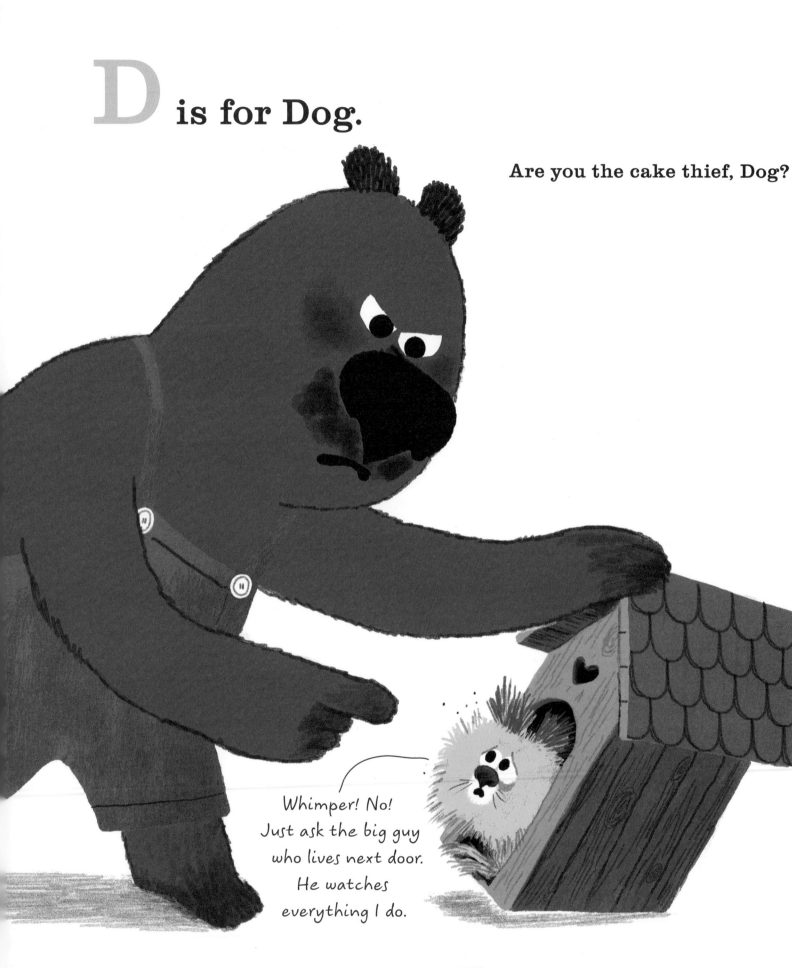

Whimper! No! Just ask the big guy who lives next door. He watches everything I do.

E is for Eye.

Hello, you big, creepy Eye. You see everything.

If only you could speak...

F is for Fox.

You've got a history of stealing sweet treats, Mr Fox. How do you plead?

It was only one tiny bite.
It was years ago.
I'm a different fox now.

G is for Gingerbread Man.

It's true, he bit me.
We all make mistakes, but I forgive Mr Fox.
We're friends now, good friends.

10

H is for Helicopter.

Hmm. Is this how the thief escaped?

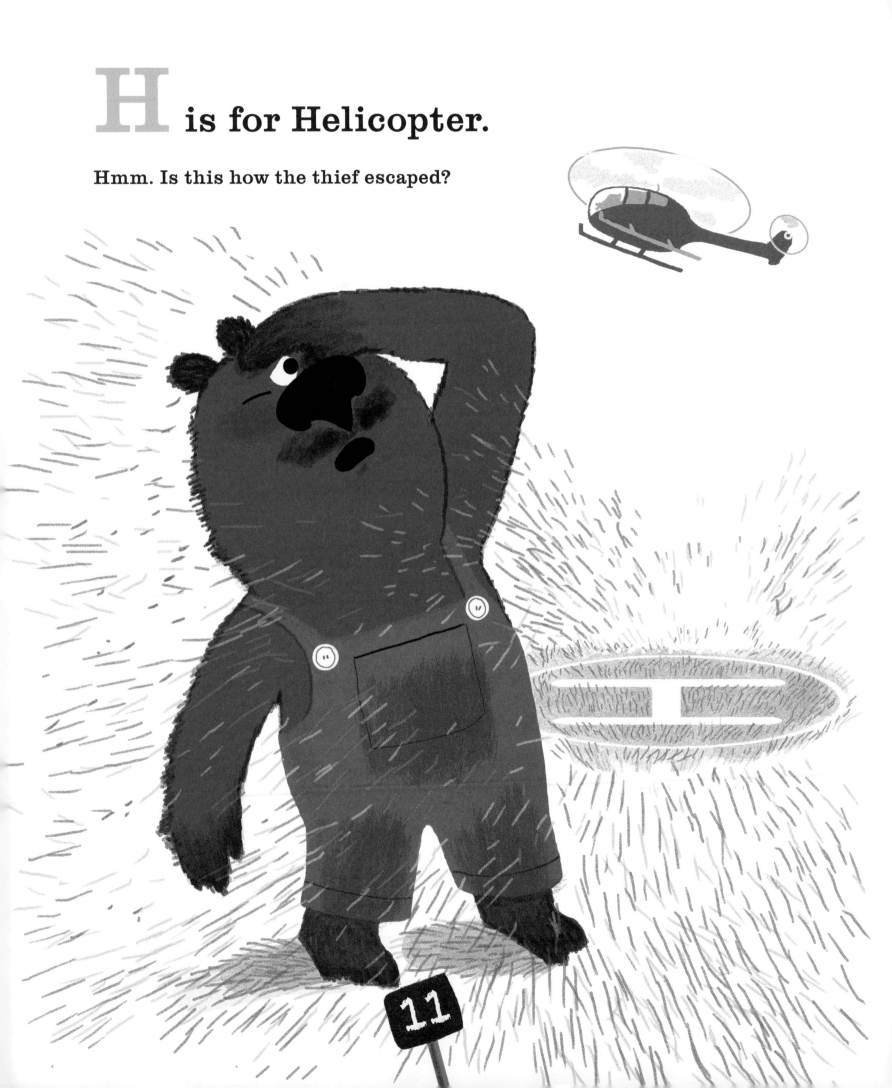

I is for Ice cream.

I'll just lick this bit to tidy it up.

J is for Jack-in-the-box.

FRIGHT!!! Oh gosh, that blasted thing gets me every time.

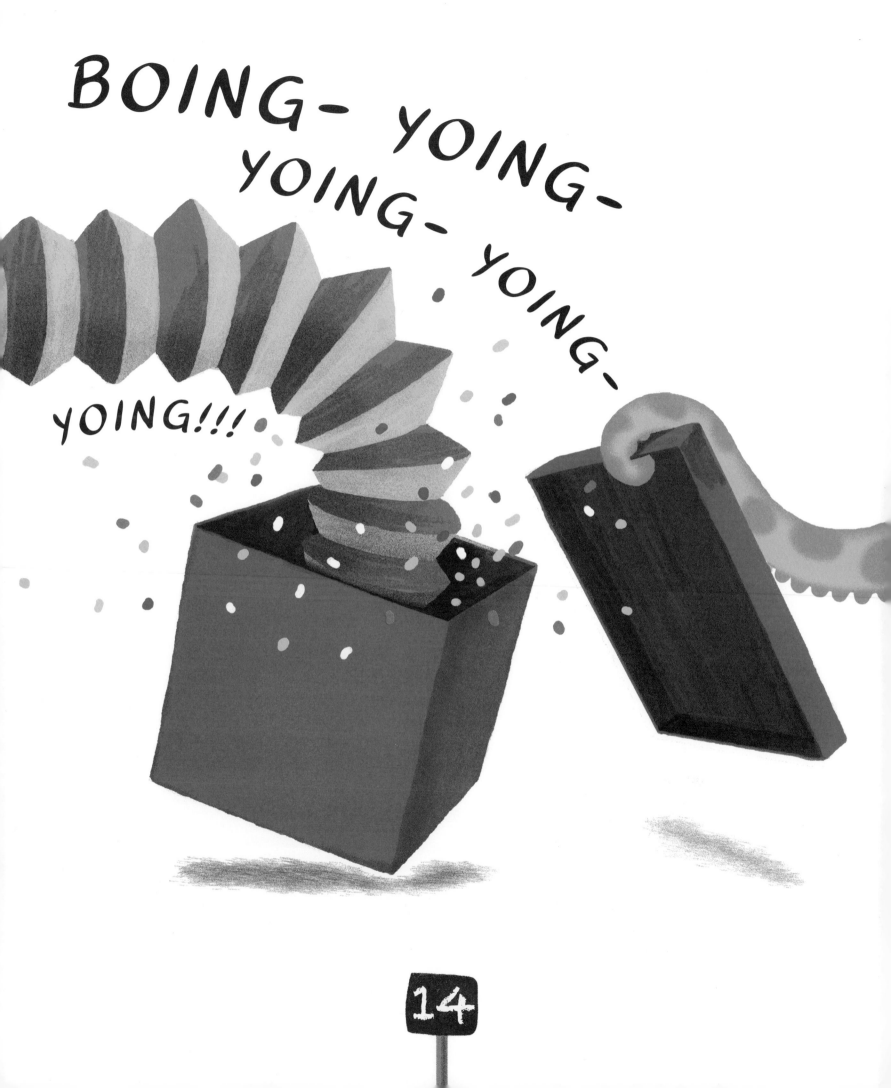

K is for Kite.

Think you're above the law?

You're coming with me, buster.

L is for Lightning.

15

M is for Mermaid.

AAAHHHHHHHHHH

NOOOOO

MY FURRRRRR!!!

N is for Nurse.

I just need to lie down for a page.

O is for Octopus.

Right! You great big Octopus...

I've seen your huge arms dangling

all over everyone else's pages.

HOW DO YOU PLEAD?!!!

You're looking rather tubby yourself today, Mr Bear. Have you put on weight?

Enough nonsense! It's time for the prime suspect...

P is for Pig.

Everyone knows you stole the cake, Pig. You're coming with me to the end of the book. For a big fat punishment.

I'm innocent!
You've got to believe me!
I didn't do it!

Tell it to the Queen, Pig.

19

Q is for Queen.

I caught him, Your Majesty.

Pig, for the crime of eating the cake,
you are banished to Page 27.
FOR EVER!

Oh, please!
Not Page 27!

20

R is for Robot.

Robot, help me escort Pig to Page 27, please.

But I have a wife!
I have a family!

21

S is for Sun.

This is the last time you'll see the sunshine for quite some time, Pig.

T is for Toothbrush.

Would you like me to brush all the crumbs out from your teeth again, Bear?

I honestly don't know what you're talking about...

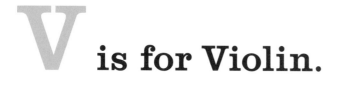

V is for Violin.

This is the end, Pig.

27

Y is for Yogurt.

Don't mind if I do...

Z is for Zip.

Think we've got this case all 'zipped up'.

Aha! Wouldn't you agree, dear reader?

What'd'ya mean? You think *I* stole the cake?

I *SAW* you eat it!

OK, you've caught me. I'm guilty. But it was just so completely deliciously, tongue-jinglingly chocolaty, all filled with cream and sprinkled with sprinkles. I just couldn't help myself ...

but this new one will be nice and safe.

Eoin McLaughlin is a picture book writer whose books include *The Hug*, illustrated by Polly Dunbar, and *Secret Agent Elephant*, illustrated by Ross Collins. When he is not writing for children, he works as a copy writer for Channel 4. Born in Ireland, Eoin has lived in Amsterdam and New York, and now lives in London with his wife and their baby. Find him on Twitter as @eoinmclaughlin.

Marc Boutavant is an award-winning graphic artist, illustrator and comic book author. He has illustrated numerous children's books, including *What Happens Next?*, written by Nicola Davies, *Edmund, The Thing*, written by Astrid Desbordes and *Never Tickle a Tiger*, written by Pamela Butchart. He is also the creator of the bestselling *Around the World with Mouk*, which has been adapted into a television series for Disney Junior UK. Born in Bourgogne, France, he now lives in Paris. Find him on Instagram as @chienpourriii.